P9-DCH-611

**Stickney-Forest View Library District**
6800 West 43rd Street
Stickney, Illinois 60402
Phone: (708)-749-1050

GAYLORD

First edition for the United States
and the Philippines published exclusively by
Barron's Educational Series, Inc. in 2001

First published in 2001
by Hodder Children's Books

**All inquiries should be addressed to:**
Barron's Educational Series, Inc.
250 Wireless Boulevard
Hauppauge, New York 11788
*http://www.barronseduc.com*°

*Library of Congress Catalog Card No.: 00-111329*

International Standard Book No.: 0-7641-1885-4

PRINTED IN HONG KONG
1 3 5 7 9 8 6 4 2

# All Change!

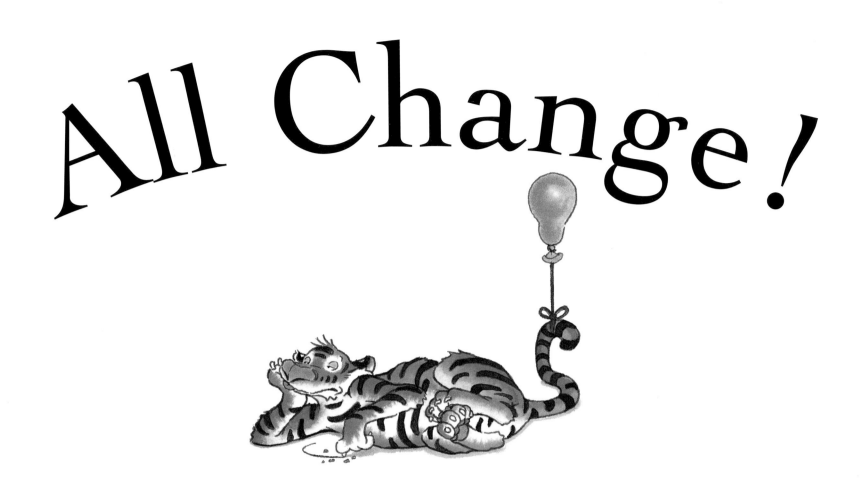

Written by Ian Whybrow

Illustrated by David Melling

BARRON'S

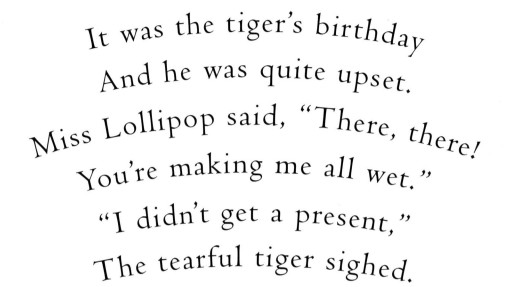

It was the tiger's birthday
And he was quite upset.
Miss Lollipop said, "There, there!
You're making me all wet."
"I didn't get a present,"
The tearful tiger sighed.

Miss Lollipop said, "Cheer up!
We'll go for a birthday ride!"

That was just what the tiger wanted
So they drove down a country lane.
Miss Lollipop shouted, "All change!"
And they jumped aboard . . .

. . . a train.

They stopped at a seashore station
And picked up a billy goat.
The goat bleated, "All change!"
So they jumped into ...

. . . a boat.

They rowed to where the seals live
And then put up the sail.
A seal barked, "All change!"
And they jumped into . . .

. . . a whale.

They rumbled in his tummy
And gave the whale a pain.
So he blew them all out through his spout
And they jumped into ...

. . . a plane.

The plane flew high up in the sky.

Then they had a bit of luck.

The pilot shouted, "All change!"
And they jumped into . . .

. . . a dump truck.

The dump truck went bumpety bump
Which is just what animals like.
The puffin shouted,
"All change!"
And they jumped onto . . .

. . . a bike.

The bell on the bike went ding, dong, ding!
But they didn't get very far.
The tiger roared out, "All change!"
And they jumped into . . .

. . . a race car.

The race car went brrrm, brrrm, brrrm,
As round the track it sped.
The animals yawned and said, "All change!"
Then they all jumped into . . .

Wait a minute, wait a minute!
What did they change into?

**Yes!** They changed into their pajamas!
Wait a minute, wait a minute!
Then what did they do?

Yes! They helped the tiger open all his presents,
And all had a piece of the tiger's birthday cake!

And then ... the animals cleaned their teeth
And this is what they said:

"Night, night, Miss Lollipop!"
And they jumped into their ...

. . . Bed!